For the mothers
and the children—
Carol, Ellen, Jamie, and Cathy
—A.D.

For my mother,
Elsie Detres Gutierrez,
a true "Night Blossom,"
who gave me the gift of
"seeing" with my heart
—R.G.

mamá and me

by **Arthur Dorros**

pictures by **Rudy Gutiérrez**

 rayo An Imprint of HarperCollins Publishers

Mamá and me are getting dressed.
"*¿Te ayudo?*" Mamá asks if I want help.
I tell her I will do it myself. "*Sola, sola.*"
There are some things only I can do.
Especially today.

First we go to the garden.
I hop ahead
and turn my face toward the sun.
"*Girasol.*" Mamá calls me sunflower.
Mamá pulls weeds. I help.
I pick flowers that Mamá likes
and save them for later.

We go into the kitchen.
I am writing, writing.
Mamá asks if I am practicing my letters.
I tell her yes.
"¿Te ayudo?" She asks if she can help me.
I tell her no, I want to do it myself.

Mamá is ready to make cookies—
our favorite, *galletas de chocolate*.
"*¿Te ayudo?*" I ask her.
"*Claro.*" Of course, she tells me.
I add more and more flour.
Mamá asks what we will do with
all those cookies.
I tell her I will eat them myself.
"*Sola, sola.*"
Mamá laughs.

Mamá looks around.

She wants to get paint to brighten the room.

I need some paint, too. I have my own idea.

"*Vámonos*," Mamá says, and we go.

I can ride my bike myself.

"*¡Sola, sola!*" says Mamá.

We find paint.

Mamá picks bright blue, for our sky, she tells me.

I pick out colors myself—reds, yellows, and greens.

"¡Me gustan!" Mamá says she likes them.

I find a great piece of cloth

and wrap it around me.

I know what I will make.

We have everything we need.

"*Al mercado.*" Mamá says we are going to the market,
so we can bring a few things to our neighbor Rosie.
I pick out the ripest mango. We smell it.
"*Dulce.*" Sweet, Mamá says.
I ask Mamá if we can buy some milk,
and I will help carry it.
"*Te ayudo,*" I tell her.

I ask Mamá to stop at Tía Elena's,

Tío Rafael's, and cousin Pablo's house.

"*Toca la puerta*," Mamá says,

and I run to the door myself, *sola, sola.*

Knock, knock, knock.

No one answers.

That's okay with me.

We stop at Rosie's.

"*¡Gracias!*" Rosie thanks us

and asks if we would like a cup of tea.

Mamá says another time,

we have painting to do.

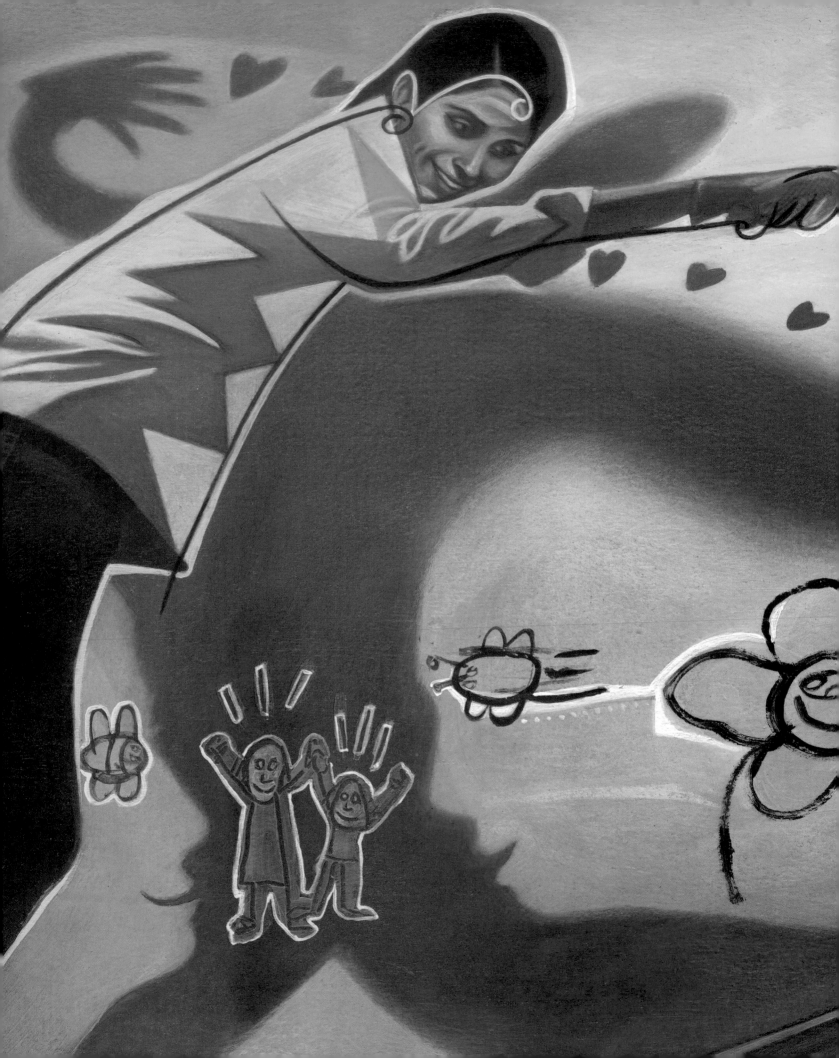

At home, we paint the walls.
Mamá makes our own sky
while I paint a garden
with birds and bugs and flowers.
"*Perfecto.*" It is perfect, says Mamá.

Now I have my own painting to do.

I paint, paint, paint in my bedroom.

Mamá calls to me, asking if I am cleaned up.

"*Pronto, pronto.*" Soon, soon, I tell her.

Finally I am ready.

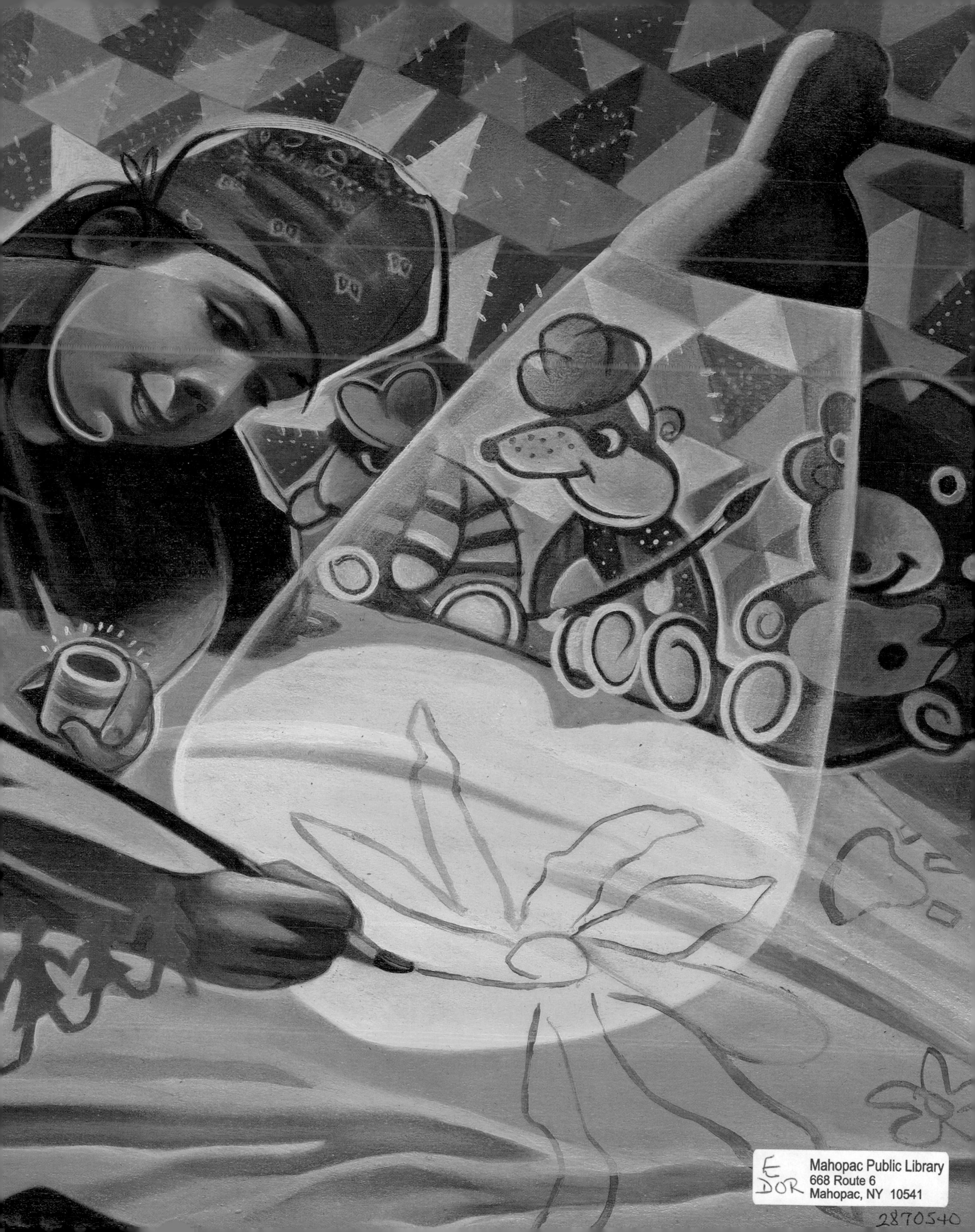

The next morning, I give Mamá my present.

"Here," I tell Mamá. "I made this myself."

"*Que lindo.*" Mamá says it is beautiful.

Then I hear knocking at the front door.

Rosie, Tía Elena, Tío Rafael,
and cousin Pablo gather round.
"¡Feliz día de las madres!"
"Happy Mother's Day," I tell Mamá
as she wraps the scarf around us.
"Sí, y mañana," Mamá says.
Tomorrow will be Mother's Day, too.